Dinosaur Christmas

by

Jerry Pallotta

CARTWHEEL BOOKS

An Imprint of Scholastic Inc.

Illustrated by

Howard McWilliam

A merry Christmas to Dr. Annekathryn Goodman.
— J.P.

For Rebecca, with love.
— H.W.

First published in 2013 by Scholastic Inc.
This edition first published in 2013 by Scholastic Children's Books
Euston House, 24 Eversholt Street
London NW1 1DB
a division of Scholastic Ltd
www.scholastic.co.uk
London ~ New York ~ Toronto ~ Sydney ~ Auckland
Mexico City ~ New Delhi ~ Hong Kong

Text copyright © Jerry Pallotta
Illustrations copyright © Howard McWilliam

ISBN 978 1407 13982 1

Dear Santa,
What did you use to pull your sleigh before you had reindeer?
Love, Jilly
x x x

Santa Claus
The Grotto
North Pole

USA

Reindeer are great at their jobs.

But I remember the good old days . . .

. . . when dinosaurs pulled my sleigh.

Triceratops were
steady and ready . . .
but a bit slow.

So I tried Parasaurolophus.

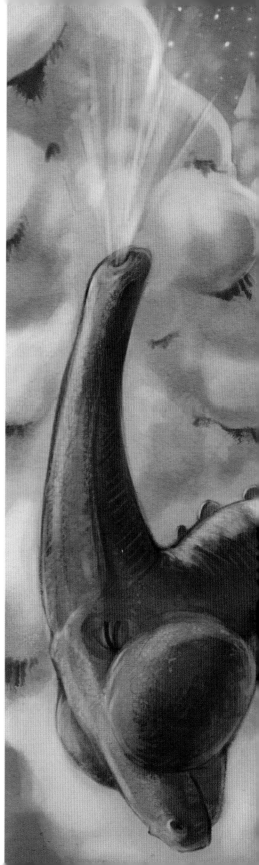

They tooted,
honked, and squeaked
too loud.

I tried Pterosaurs.
They flew so high.
Help! I couldn't breathe.

And those Velociraptors.

They were fidgety. *Stop slashing at each other!*

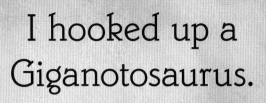

I hooked up a
Giganotosaurus.

It was a gigantic-o
mistake-o!

And those Tyrannosaurus rex . . .

They wouldn't
stop licking me!

The Maiasauras were pretty and well behaved.

Until they ate the presents.
Bad dinosaurs!
I'm telling your mother!

Oh! And those Styracosaurus.

Pushy and *way* too bossy.

Then I tried
Stegosaurus.

It was a merry, spiky,
pointy Christmas.

I tried Gallimimus.

They wouldn't stop dancing.

The Apatosaurus
worked well.

They were great
for deliveries and
seeing ahead.

Ankylosaurus,
Zephyrosaurus,
Nodosaurus —
they never bored us.

Today the dinosaurs are gone.

Now the reindeer are my helpers.
And they're a treasure.

But sometimes
I miss the
good old days.

Merry
Christmas!